For my "Ozzie", the greatest little salesman I know!

TOYS FOR SALE!

WRITTEN AND ILLUSTRATED BY: HEATHER GILBERT

Toys for sale! Toys for sale! I have oodles and doodles of toys for sale!

I've cleaned out my room. Yes, I've gone through my stuff. I agree with my mom when she says that I have "quite enough"

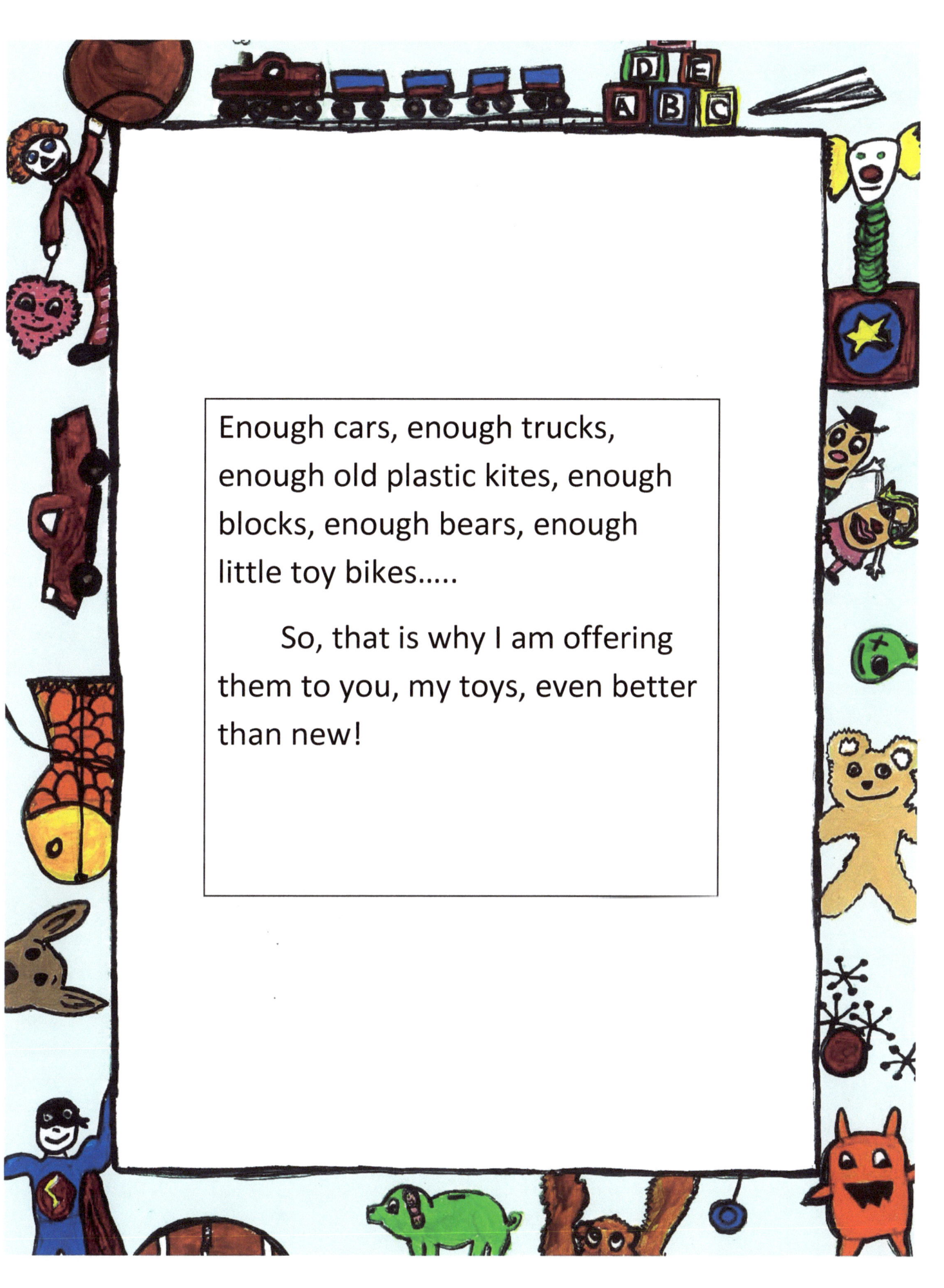

Enough cars, enough trucks, enough old plastic kites, enough blocks, enough bears, enough little toy bikes.....

So, that is why I am offering them to you, my toys, even better than new!

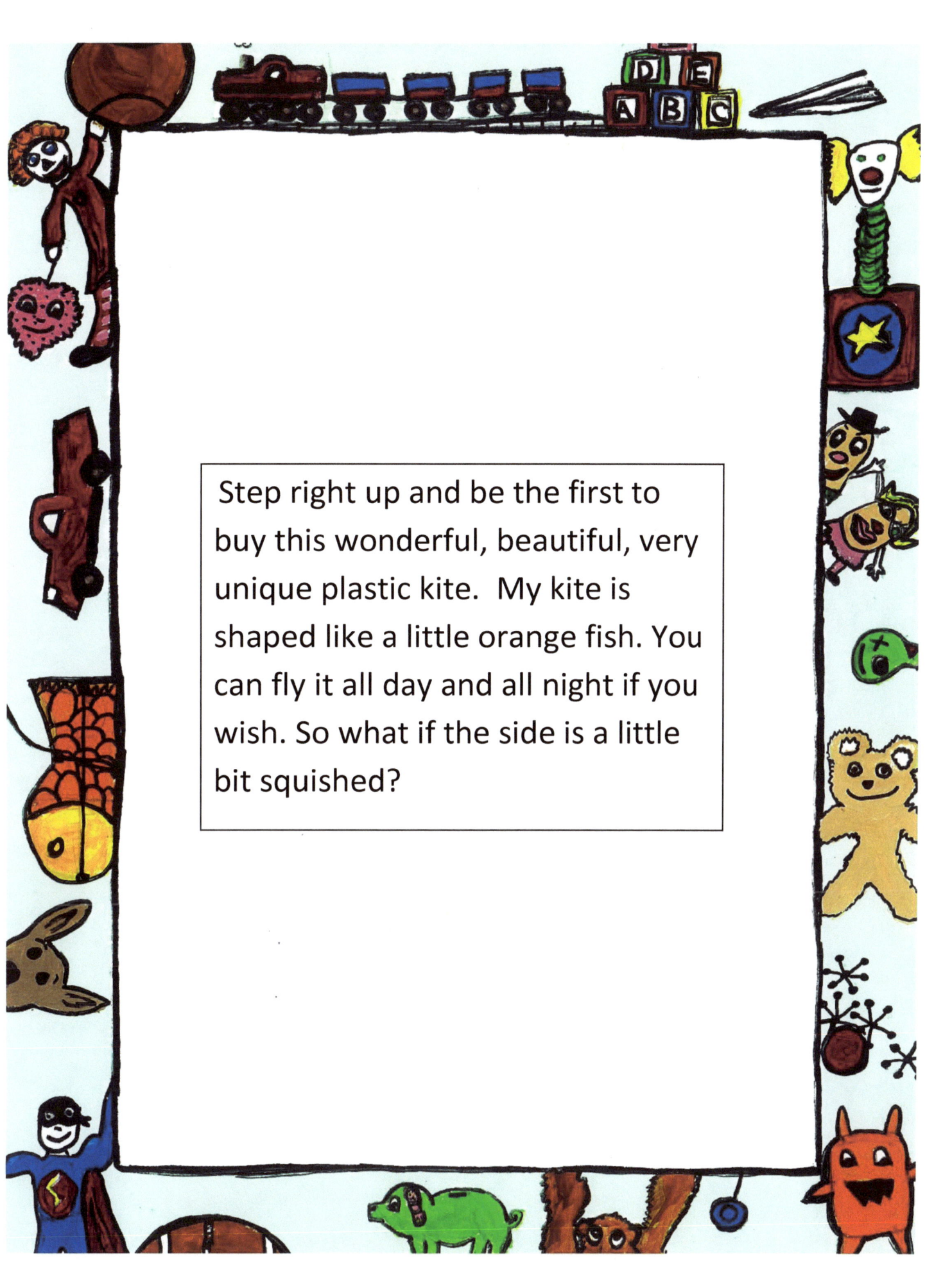

Step right up and be the first to buy this wonderful, beautiful, very unique plastic kite. My kite is shaped like a little orange fish. You can fly it all day and all night if you wish. So what if the side is a little bit squished?

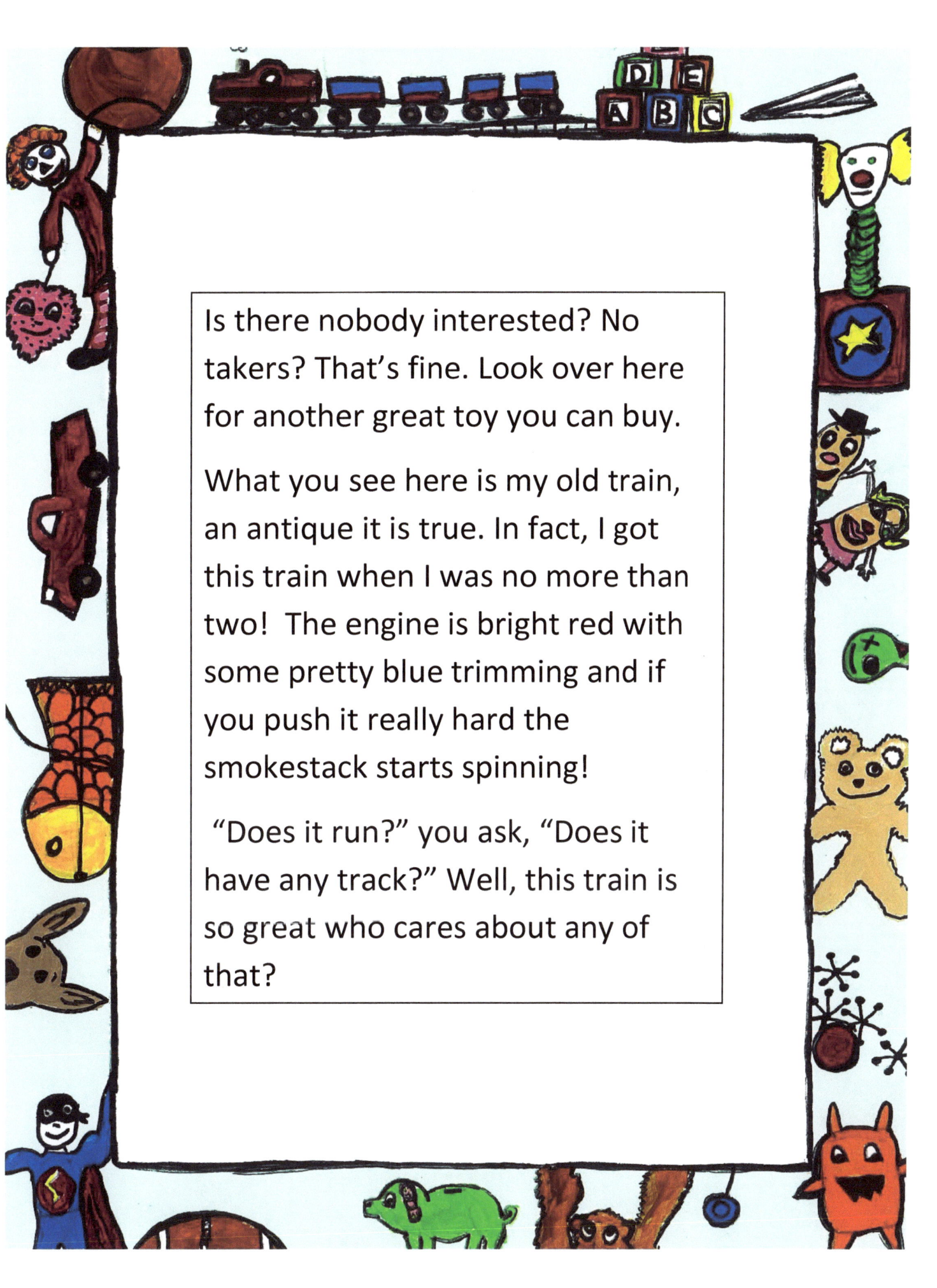

Is there nobody interested? No takers? That's fine. Look over here for another great toy you can buy.

What you see here is my old train, an antique it is true. In fact, I got this train when I was no more than two! The engine is bright red with some pretty blue trimming and if you push it really hard the smokestack starts spinning!

"Does it run?" you ask, "Does it have any track?" Well, this train is so great who cares about any of that?

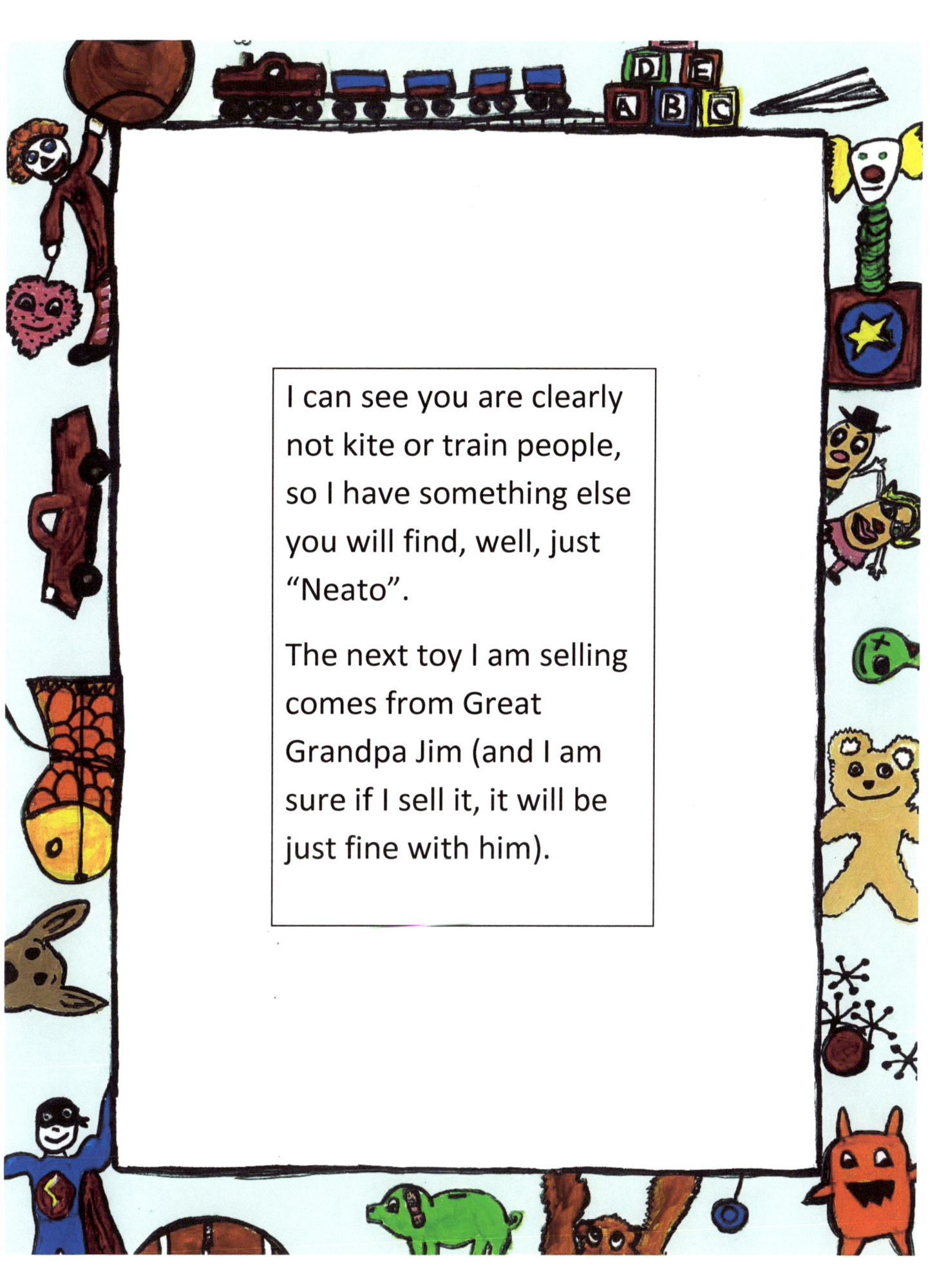

I can see you are clearly not kite or train people, so I have something else you will find, well, just "Neato".

The next toy I am selling comes from Great Grandpa Jim (and I am sure if I sell it, it will be just fine with him).

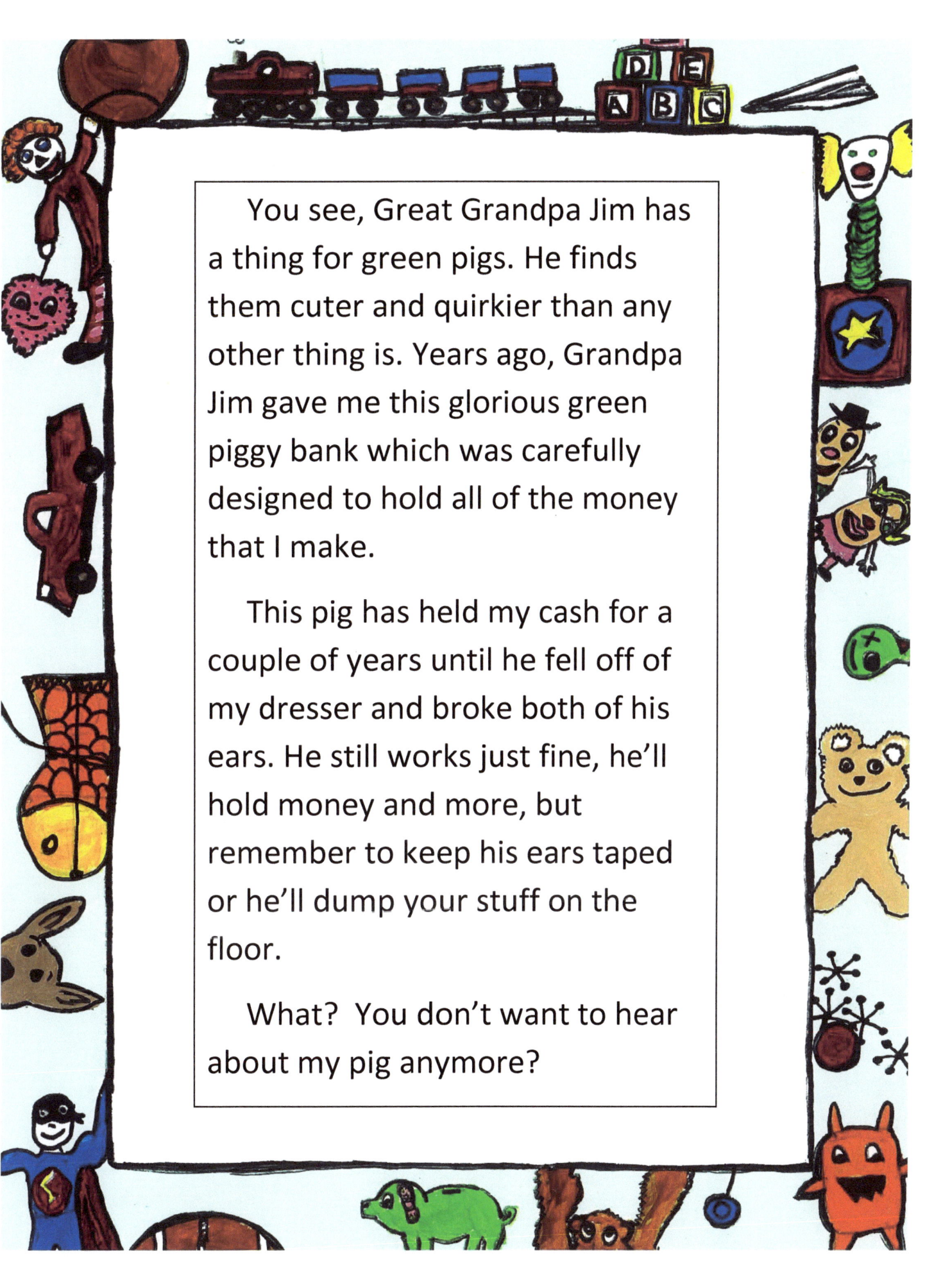

You see, Great Grandpa Jim has a thing for green pigs. He finds them cuter and quirkier than any other thing is. Years ago, Grandpa Jim gave me this glorious green piggy bank which was carefully designed to hold all of the money that I make.

This pig has held my cash for a couple of years until he fell off of my dresser and broke both of his ears. He still works just fine, he'll hold money and more, but remember to keep his ears taped or he'll dump your stuff on the floor.

What? You don't want to hear about my pig anymore?

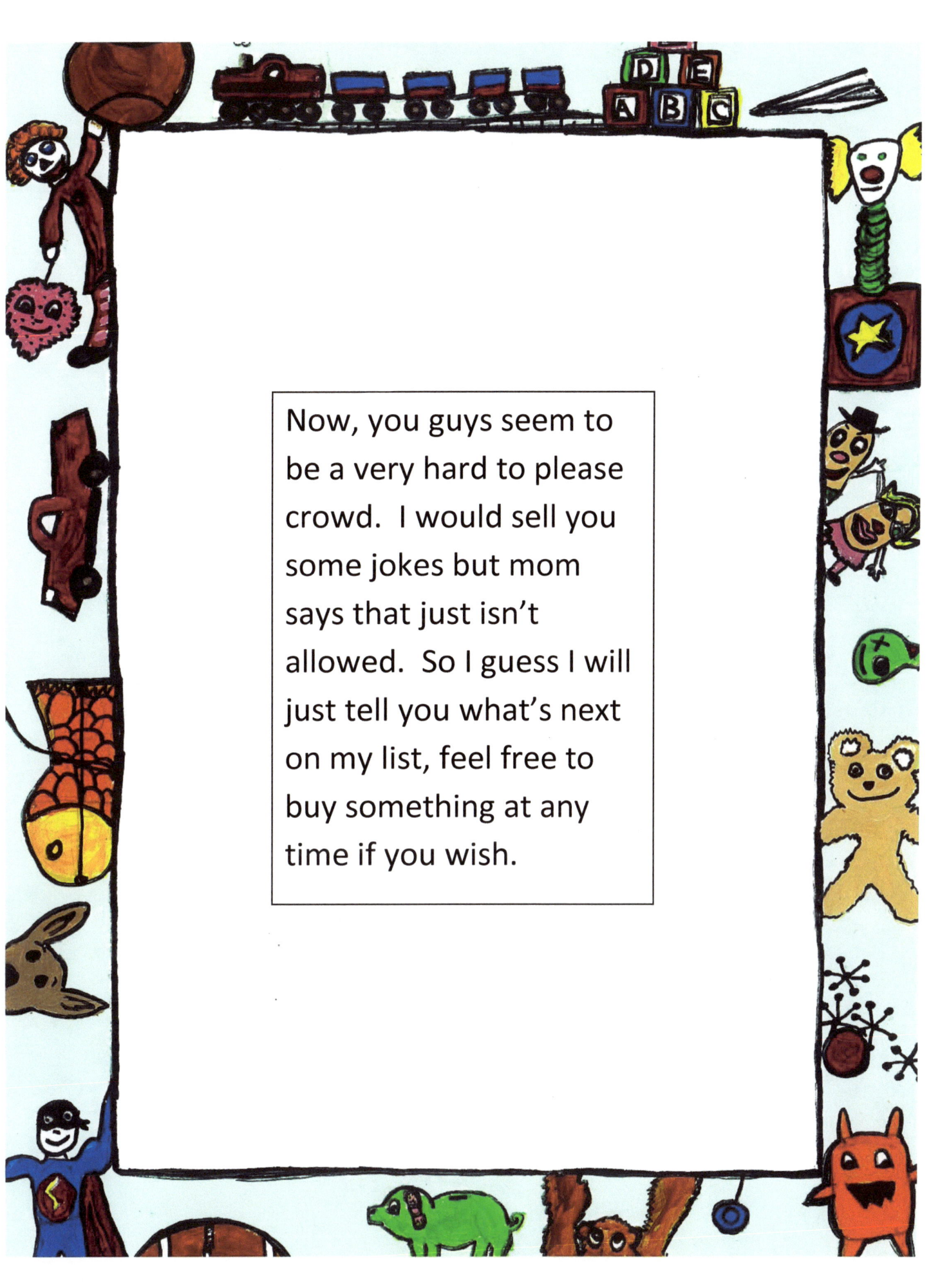

Now, you guys seem to be a very hard to please crowd. I would sell you some jokes but mom says that just isn't allowed. So I guess I will just tell you what's next on my list, feel free to buy something at any time if you wish.

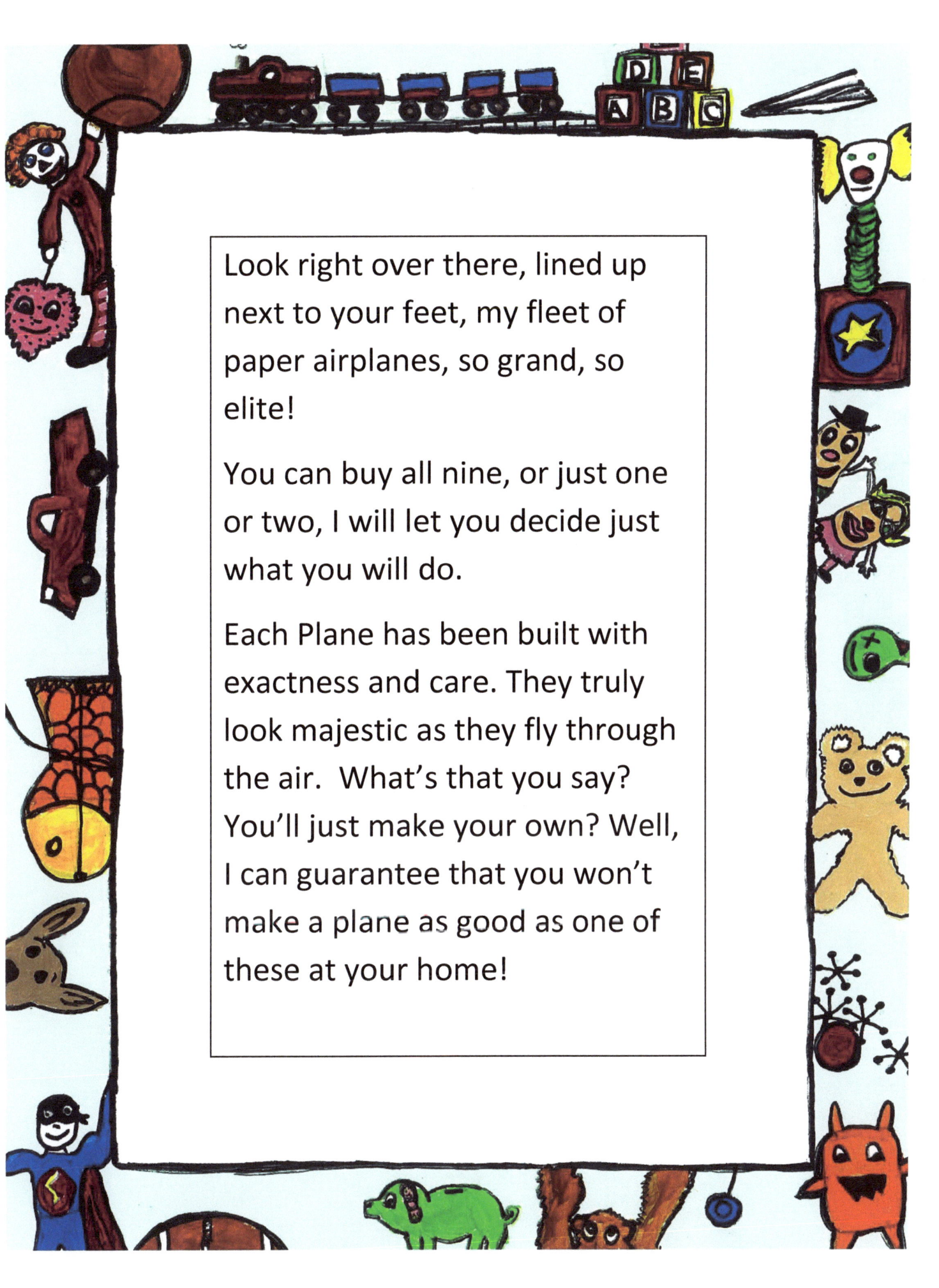

Look right over there, lined up next to your feet, my fleet of paper airplanes, so grand, so elite!

You can buy all nine, or just one or two, I will let you decide just what you will do.

Each Plane has been built with exactness and care. They truly look majestic as they fly through the air. What's that you say? You'll just make your own? Well, I can guarantee that you won't make a plane as good as one of these at your home!

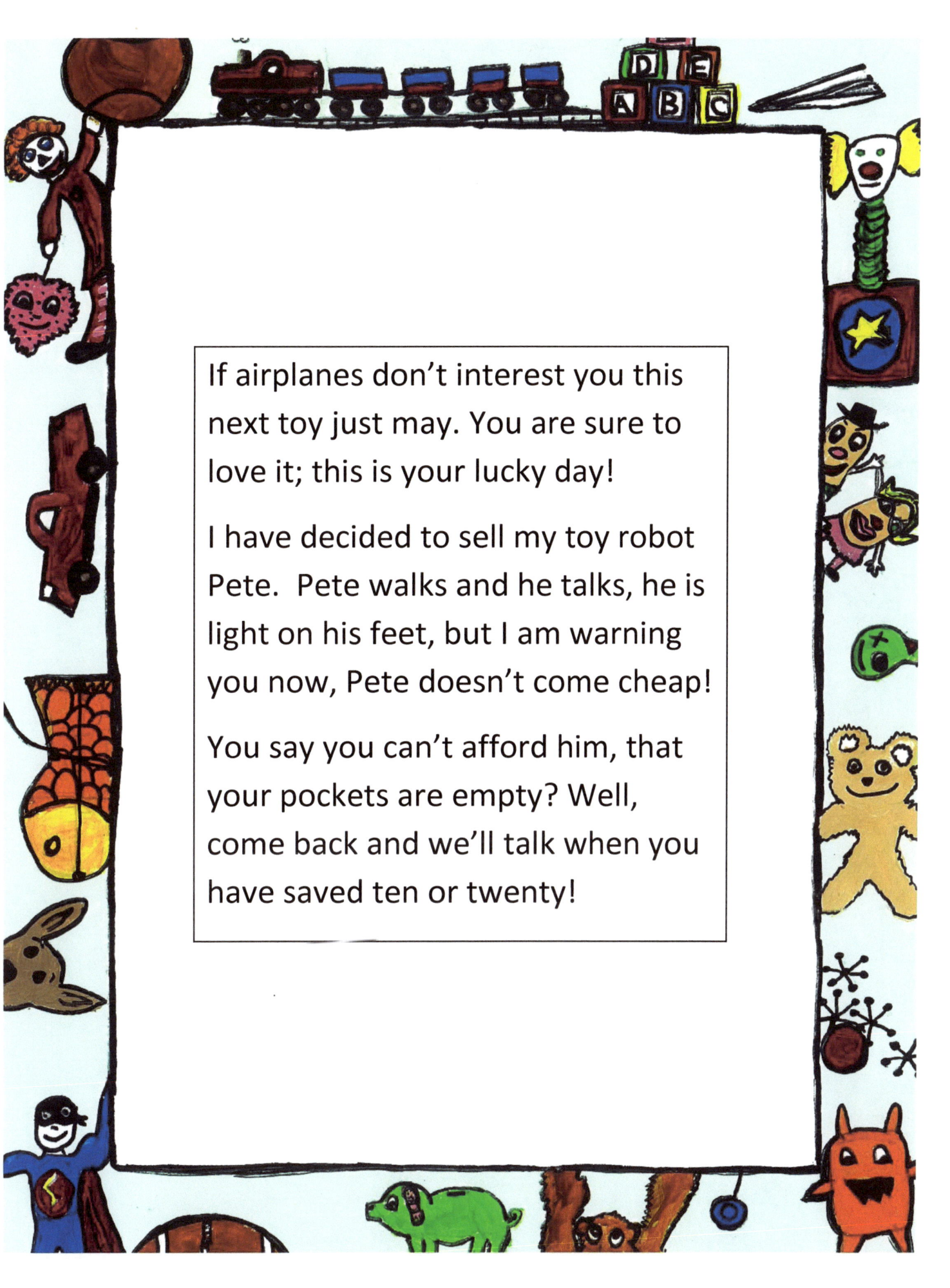

If airplanes don't interest you this next toy just may. You are sure to love it; this is your lucky day!

I have decided to sell my toy robot Pete. Pete walks and he talks, he is light on his feet, but I am warning you now, Pete doesn't come cheap!

You say you can't afford him, that your pockets are empty? Well, come back and we'll talk when you have saved ten or twenty!

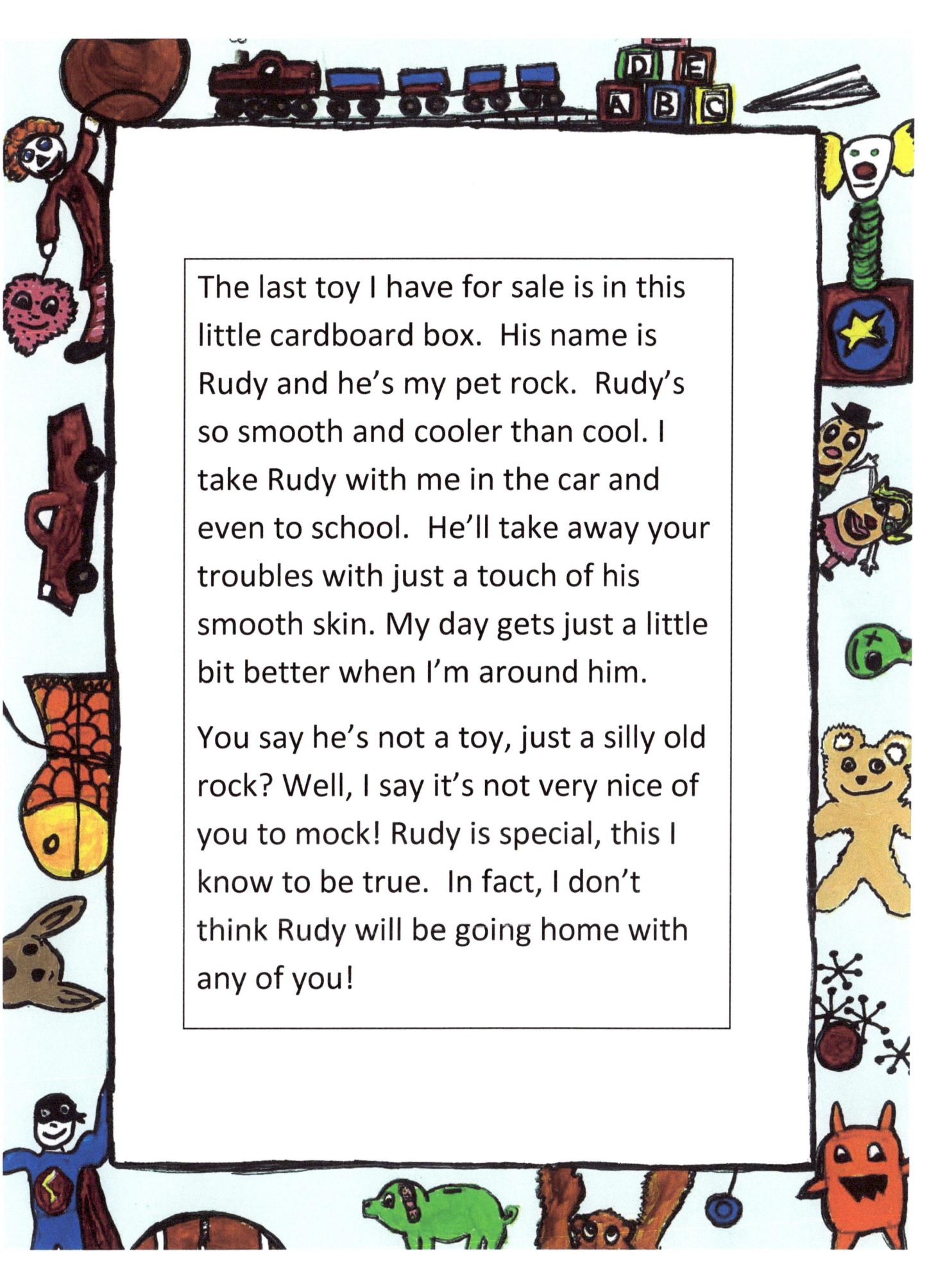

The last toy I have for sale is in this little cardboard box. His name is Rudy and he's my pet rock. Rudy's so smooth and cooler than cool. I take Rudy with me in the car and even to school. He'll take away your troubles with just a touch of his smooth skin. My day gets just a little bit better when I'm around him.

You say he's not a toy, just a silly old rock? Well, I say it's not very nice of you to mock! Rudy is special, this I know to be true. In fact, I don't think Rudy will be going home with any of you!

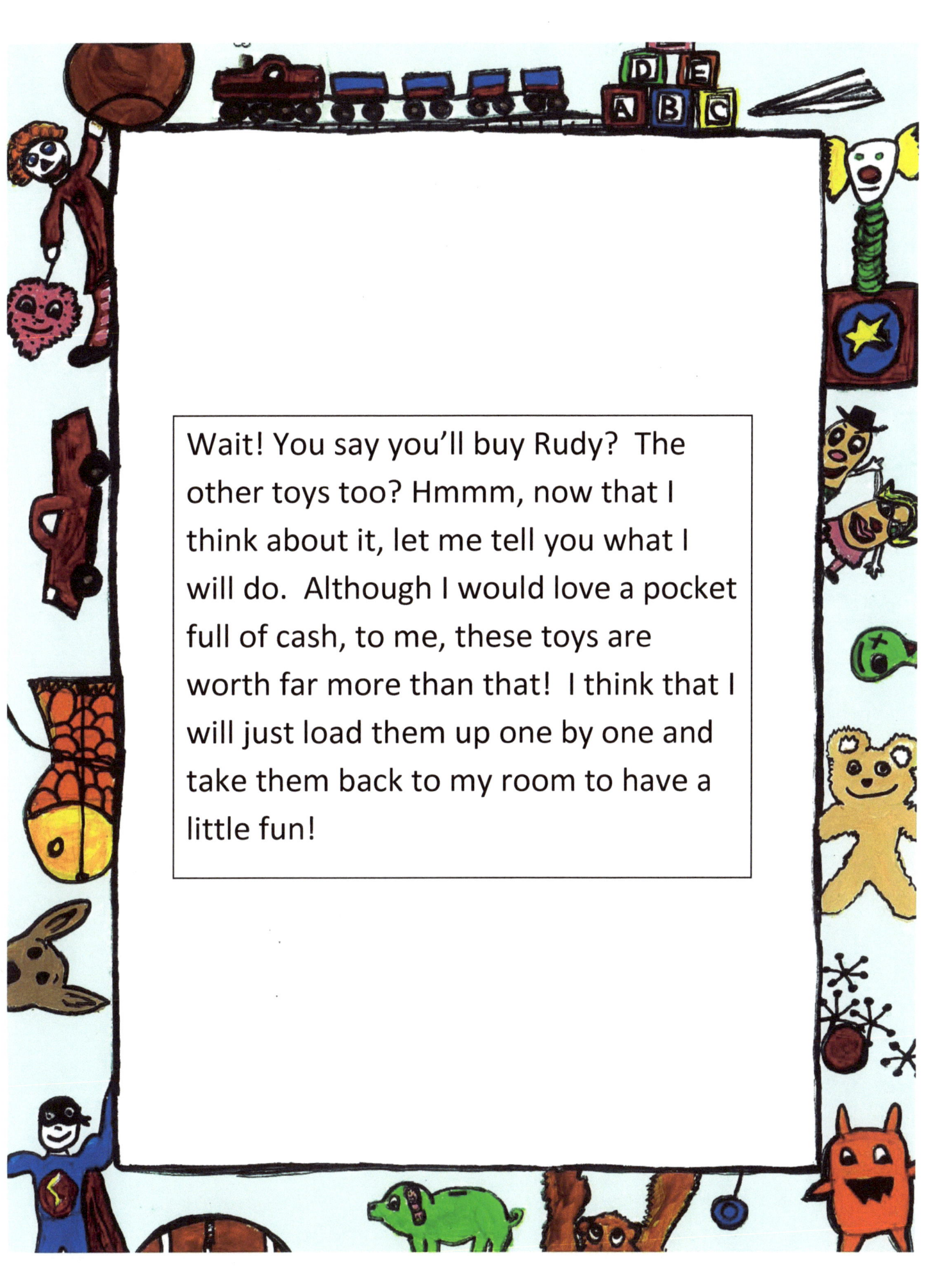

Wait! You say you'll buy Rudy? The other toys too? Hmmm, now that I think about it, let me tell you what I will do. Although I would love a pocket full of cash, to me, these toys are worth far more than that! I think that I will just load them up one by one and take them back to my room to have a little fun!